THIS BOOK BELONGS TO

FOR EDDIE AND BILL WITH LOVE —PF

TO DENISE AND LOUISE —RJ

First US edition 2022
First published by Walker Books Ltd. (UK) 2022

Library of Congress Catalog Card Number pending
ISBN 978-1-5362-2852-6

22 23 24 25 26 27 APS 10 9 8 7 6 5 4 3 2 1

Printed in Humen, Dongguan, China

This book was typeset in Chaparral Pro.
The illustrations were done in mixed media.

Candlewick Press
99 Dover Street
Somerville, Massachusetts 02144

www.candlewick.com

Through the North Pole Snow

POLLY FABER ILLUSTRATED BY RICHARD JONES

CANDLEWICK PRESS

A little fox came hunting through the snow.

It was trying to find something—anything—for dinner.

Everywhere was so cold.

Everywhere was so dark.

Hop! Hop!

Thump!

Again and again, it sprang up and
punched down into the thick white blanket.

In some places, the ground was too hard and the snow too shallow.

In other places, the ground was too soft and the snow too deep.

But in one place . . .

Ah!

The little fox saw light and color

and felt warmth again.

And the little fox smelled dinner, so it kept digging.

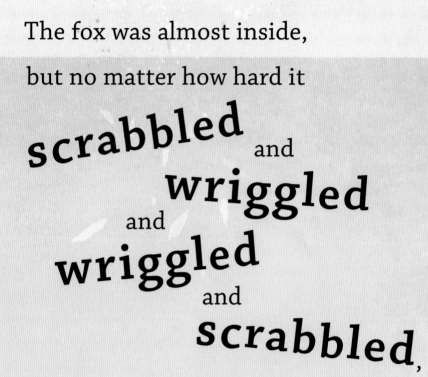

The fox was almost inside,

but no matter how hard it

scrabbled and

wriggled

and

wriggled

and

scrabbled,

it couldn't get through.

Then a voice said, "Stuck? Now that's a problem I understand!"

Two hands took hold
of the little fox
and pulled.

The hands belonged to a man with a great round belly and a fox-white beard. He looked very old and very tired but so kind that the little fox wasn't frightened.

"Help yourself to dinner. There's plenty left over; I was already full of cookies," the old man said, and he gave a yawn and went to bed.

By the light of the giant log burning
on the fire, the little fox explored.

There were snowy boots and steaming clothes.
There were piles of paper everywhere.
And there were rows and rows of empty shelves.

Eventually the fox grew tired and went to bed.

On
and
on
the man slept.
The little fox slept,
too, some of
the time.

Until one day a shaft of sunlight shone through
the hole in the ceiling, and the man sat up with a stretch.
He smiled when he saw the little fox: "You're still here?"
The man didn't look so old now.

With the world lit bright again,
the little fox played outside and found flowers,
chased insects, and followed streams.

Sometimes
the man came, too,
but mostly now
he was busy.

He drew and measured and made plans.

He sawed and painted and hammered.

And he cut and sewed and stuffed.

And slowly,

slowly,

he filled up all the empty shelves from their tops
to their bottoms.

When the sun began to sink away once more
and the first snow arrived, something else fell with it:
letters. They floated through the sky. Hundreds,
then thousands of them.

The little fox helped the man find every single one.

Then the man read and he read.

He made lists.

He matched the lists to things on the shelves,

adding notes and crossing things off.

And he filled a great sack. He didn't stop until . . .

colored lights came dancing across the sky and eight reindeer arrived.
Pawing and snorting and steaming, they dipped their heads for silver
bells to be tied to their antlers and were harnessed to a sleigh.

"Coming, little fox?" asked the man.

His eyes sparkled brighter than snow.

The little fox went,

and, at last, understood everything.

And when the sleigh was empty,
the fox's heart was full.

And together, the fox and Santa Claus came home.